Amuráti

(One-Page Shorts)

VOLUME ONE
FIFTY SHORT STORIES

By
Amurá Oñaā

Published by

UNLIMITED LLC
2017

A work of fiction. All of the characters and names are products of the author's imagination or used fictitiously.

ISBN 978-0-578-19410-3
AMURÁTI (ONE-PAGE SHORTS, VOLUME 1)

Cover Design and Art by Amurá Oñaā

Published by Amurá Unlimited, LLC

Introduction

After the first story, which I had placed in a body of work called Passing Thoughts to post on Facebook, I went to bed, and sometime before deep sleep took hold, the idea of One-Page Shorts came to me. I'd like to treat it as a form of short story writing in the way writers treat haiku as a form of poetic verse. It would be a story on a page within a 300-word parameter (for English, different considerations for different languages). I deleted my FB post and changed it to One-Page Shorts. Still, whether or not the idea is a novel one or whether others did it elsewhere is unimportant to me, it's novel to me.

I have bequeathed these One-Page Shorts, "Amuráti" (being singular or plural), a literary work specifically written to have 300 words or less in the English tongue. Translated stories may wind up slightly longer; it will be allowable as long as they meet the parameters of the language the author wrote. Why "Amuráti"? — My name Amurá means "one flame," and so it feels appropriate that readers treat these stories as a flicker, a wisp, a small snippet of life.

The stories carry no titles. The responsibility of providing titles falls on the shoulders of the reader. Page numbers for the stories are also non-existent as the stories themselves incorporate the folio. A story can become known as "Story XXV of Volume 1," and so on. Currently, there are no groupings, no underlying themes or styles in this publication. The stories are in the order they came: hopefully, there will be many still waiting in line.

While this may be my first published literary work, I've come to realize that, with diaries, poetry, game rules, and song lyrics, I've been writing virtually all my life. I understand that if nothing else comes out of this experience, I feel blessed with the joy of putting pen to paper; a pleasure I expect to continue to experience, I hope you enjoy the ride along with me. I offer my thanks to those who only asked me, "Why haven't you published anything yet?"

I

She looked, but the filth on her window clouded her view.

She swore she saw a child hauntingly familiar.

Reaching in her apron pocket for a paper towel, she spits and quickly wiped for clarity.

She felt her heart racing-a-pace for a long-forgotten yesterday.

Faster, she had to wipe more quickly!

She cupped her old hands like binoculars, eyes fixated, and pressing hard, she could feel the window strain.

Shouting out in a voice only she could hear, "Jesus! I do know that child!"

Just then, the small girl turned and gazed back. She suddenly remembered that Saturday, so long ago, when some crazy old lady was looking at her through a gray, dirty window.

II

He told her that he had nothing to do with the robbery.

She cradled their whining, two-year-old son in her arms, trying her best to adjust him as small arms flailed her face and legs pushed against her as if he wanted to fall.

She paced the kitchen floor, yelling at the air in the room, "Then why were the damn police here twice? Twice!"

He was too tired, too tired to hear her shit having already spent four and a half stressful hours at the precinct.

He didn't want to fight; he needed his sleep. Just to shut up the noise crashing down all around him. The cops, his wife, the baby, the day, he would tell her anything. Anything!

"Hon, I think I know who it was. I'll go to the cops in the morning." He meant nothing by it, but his resolved look shook her to her core.

"Damn it; you do that. I can't take this crap. You and those damn fools you hang with!" Still, she wasn't sure as to how much he knew.

"Now here, finish your tea, I'll wake you later," she said, handing him a cup.

He finished his tea, looked at his wife, who finally got the baby quiet, smiled and slumped over dead.

His wife called the neighborhood precinct, "Can I speak to Detective Miller? I'll wait."

"Hello, honey, Nick's dead. I just couldn't take the chance. I think he might have known about us, the robbery and maybe even about that child is yours. Can you come and get rid of the body?

"You're such a doll. Love ya. Bye."

III

He nervously approached his tenement building on his way back. It would be way too hard to tell his mother the "whole" truth. He had to be selective; there needed to be "choice" within the details.

He needed only specifics he could quickly memorize and repeat without any of the quirks or body ticks that so often betrayed him. He would love to "place blame," but baby sis was too young and out with dad.

Mom had a way about her, leaving him little to no way. Each suspense-filled step he took to the top floor would find him shaking, but determined. Still, the higher he climbed, the lower he sunk.

Then it hit him, "The Bundle," his old ace in a hole. That's it—he would bundle little lies together, no more than seven to ten, keeping them in sequence.

He began practicing the order of events, stopping every so often to correct himself. Yes, he would be ready by the time he hit the sixth floor.

To his surprise, mom popped out of a neighbor's apartment on the fourth floor. He was so startled. The shock blew his bundle to pieces, as he almost pissed on himself.

"Mom, I did it," it just came out. "I broke the lamp with the basketball." Tears near the edge of his eyelids, ready to make the leap.

"Oh, honey, I haven't been home yet. But thanks for telling me, didn't like that ugly old lamp anyhow. Now I can get something I like. Give me some sugar." She hugged him and kissed him on his forehead.

It didn't matter whether she was honest with him or not. She always knew just what to say.

He squeezed her, saying with relief, "God, I love you, Mom."*

*Written on Mother's Day 2017.

IV

They knew the hideous dragon would come: it was that season of the year in a cycle unchanged for decades. All they could do was prepare themselves, store away what they could, sharpen what weapons they had, and repair traps that never entirely did the job.

Prayers recited at gatherings where many attended shrouded in memories of dark, dreary yesterdays. There was no venturing out at night this time of year.

At sunrise of "Dragon's Day," a wounded knight on horseback appeared asking to be allowed in. They raised the gate, but, as the knight's mighty steed reached the town square, he crumbled from his horse, holding the feared dragon's head in a sack.

A mass of people gathered around him, tended to his wounds, and praised his deeds. Just then, the village idiot came running out and, for a crazy instant, tried to break up their celebration.

Shouting repeatedly, "Keep the head on holy ground,

> Never let it dwell in town,
> Curse be born to town with head,
> Dragon rise, and all fall dead.
> Take my heed, begone you, clowns."

"Get out of here, you 'ol maggot!" they screamed.

They took the knight to an inn to better treat his injuries. He could not thank them as his words became garbled, and his face turned gruesome and distorted. Suddenly they noticed, in the places showing skin, large scales appeared and quickly multiplied.

He rose and roared, throwing everyone back against the wall. There was a blinding light followed by equally blinding darkness at midday. The inn was no more, and in its place stood a towering dragon slaughtering town folk.

All were gone but for the village idiot, who fled into the forest path, singing that limerick, taking the shape of a grotesque, dwarfish dragon.

V

They sat across from each other on the earthen floor as the season's hard rain patted loudly. Yet just above the din of the downpour was a silence. Mother and daughter - each wrestled with a sense of emptiness.

Shanisa would glance at her mother every so often from the lappa Shanisa was mending to see how much her mother's eyes would reveal. While the flickering light from the small fire in the far corner danced all over Niana's round face, the eyes remained fixed downward on the flat, stone slab with the dough she had been meticulously kneading, and so they offered Shanisa little comfort.

Finally, a soft, tired sigh emptied passed Niana's lips: she took a moment to stare out through the window. "Alright," she said, breaking their silence, "while there is no memory of this kind of event in my day or the days of our ancestors, I'm willing to accept this change along with other changes to come if it's meant to be so."

"Not much will change after I'm gone," Shanisa needed to add. "They promised to return us."

"But when?" Niana asked, "When?"

"When this world needs us." She grabbed her mother in her arms, each shedding tears.

Shanisa stepped out into the village circle, where others of her age had gathered and waited. The rains had dissipated, and other families surrounded them.

When Shanisa reached them, they joined hands, and Shanisa pressed the bracelet on her arm. Eyes shared a farewell with their families. Finally, a large air vehicle arrived, hovered over them, and shined down a light beam. They were lifted into the craft, and it sped away to the stars as her mother watched.

In her people's oral history, they would remember them as "Those who left to return."

VI

She had watched her father abuse, terrorize, and disrespect her mother far too many times in her young life. She was reaching a point in her life where her coloring of men fell into grays with dull-blunted textures. Now she was reaching an age where her father's gaze became increasingly alarming; it was a gaze of opportunity, something she was not prepared for and felt she had to get away from her father.

One night he came home intoxicated and sat in her room watching her play. As she got up, he grabbed her arm and pulled her to him, as if sizing up her ripeness. "Aren't you gonna say hello to your Daddy?" He smiled glaringly.

"Yes, hi, Daddy," she was able to meek out.

He released her with a pat on her rump. Maybe she wasn't quite what he wanted yet, or perhaps it was the look her mother gave him from down the hallway.

The next day she found herself on a train, with one large suitcase, going cross country to live with Aunt Sylvia. She loved her aunt, had nick-named her Aunt Sylvi. The closest to calling her Aunt Silly and remain respectful.

Her room was ready by the time she got there. She sat quietly at the kitchen table while her aunt made her a cup of hot chocolate. Sylvi gently kissed her head, "Don't worry, everything that can be done has been done."

She wondered what her aunt meant by that as she watched Sylvi putting away a few enchanted objects she always had around the house along with a small male doll.

Aunt Sylvi turned and added, "Life will always teach you what you need to learn!"

In a month, her mother wrote, Dad had a nervous breakdown and wouldn't be coming home.

VII

They waited. The soldiers dug in. The gunfire and firefight that forced them to their present position were still raging as their comrades, and the newly arrived aliens fought in a clearing behind them. They had no idea who they were.

One planet too many, Brian thought, unhitching his ammo pack to get a better count of what remained.

Still, whoever they were, this planet indeed wasn't theirs, it was up for grabs, at least that's what he thought. After all, the indigenous inhabitants were primitives; with obviously no idea of the amount of wealth in natural resources, this planet could offer the Fleet or any other space-faring civilization.

We had arrived four days ago before these adversaries came, and now it was a fight to the death. Brian's team moved deeper into the tall foliage for cover with the enemy close behind.

The air unexpectedly changed color as the plants around them began to release massive amounts of toxic pollen. The men around him, along with the aliens, started collapsing, suffocating to death. Brian attached his helmet, but it was slowly melting along with his uniform.

Some primitives arrived in what appeared to be protective garments. Brian fell to his knees: he turned on his universal translator.

The primitive closest to him said, "I am sorry for you and those who would harm you, but our plants have a mind that will not allow your kind of violence to exist here. We would've gladly shared with you both, but it appears that sharing is not your way."

Brian laid there, dying, confused, but in awe.

VIII

As the rightful, next-in-line ruler of his kingdom, he had grown quite accustomed to expect what would and naturally should be his—the crown. So being deceitful, arrogant, and one to quickly exaggerate his deeds, it really didn't matter to him. His course was charted and supported by those willing to accept his bribes.

There was only one problem—the king would not die. The young king-to-be crafted fabricated tales of how the king was plotting against him and that there were spies in the palace with ears the size of northern wolves.

Surely he should be king by now! Was he not the better man as always, he told himself? Time stitched too many years together.

Finally, he went to the Queen-Mother, his actual mother, and confessed his total disbelief as to his father's longevity!

His mother rose quietly from her bed and stood before her son. Her eyes went deep into him, a look he had long forgotten. In quiet strength, she told him what few others had the courage to, "You, my son, are a liar, a harbinger of deceit, one who cannot be honest with yourself, let alone our people."

"I have been giving this magical elixir to your father, an honest man."

"I have never lied; it's not in me to do such a thing!" he protested.

"Then drink the elixir as an honest man can!" She pushed it toward him. He reached for it.

"Of course, it is deadly to those who lie," she added.

Hesitant, with eyes searching for an escape, he pushed the elixir aside, left the room, the country, and was never heard of again.

IX

On her deathbed, grandma motioned for her two daughters to come closer. She brought their hands together. She wrapped her gold chain necklace around their hands, placed her hand on top of theirs, and patted them, saying, "There's power in this!" She then closed her eyes for the last time.

They pulled their hands away. The older sister presuming the necklace was meant for her, took it. Her sister gave her a questioning look but said nothing—certain they wouldn't speak again for a long time.

One day her mother was visiting her eldest daughter and found her swearing and cursing at the necklace. "There is no power in this! Grandma lied to us!" She shook it in her mother's face and said, "Give this to your other daughter." She refused even to say her name.

"Only if you come with me," her mother insisted.

When they arrived, the younger daughter didn't want it, didn't want to have anything to do with it or her sister.

The mother asked them precisely what did Nana say and do, as she was in another village and had not been able to attend.

After they finished their tale, their mother looked at them shaking her head. "Pathetic, you two are pathetic."

They questioned her response.

"This necklace is nothing but a binder and only a binder. Nana was telling you that the power is in the both of you. Staying together, working together, that there's power in the family, not this trinket!"

Both daughters sat, ashamed, humiliated, and unable to speak. Overcoming their differences would take time, but they knew they needed to learn from their mistakes.

X

The jury was in, and they pronounced his innocence. He was shaken to tears as he hugged his lawyers, not so much because the man was genuinely innocent but because he was guilty as a pig in a sty. He knew his lawyers knew, but a technicality was all he needed.

He looked across the courtroom only to see the disdain in the eyes of the people he defrauded out of millions. If hatred were a peanut butter sandwich, it'd be sticking to the roof of your mouth, something his kid brother always said and was saying right now as he turned to hug him.

"You are one lucky son of a b…"

"You're just saying that cause I'm better lookin'," he interjected.

"Crazy like a fox. Let's get out of this damn courtroom. The vibes are giving me the willies!"

"There's a bar across the avenue; I could use a cold one. One sec," he said, feeling a shiver run up his spine, waking from his sleep.

"So just how many times are you going to dream that dream?" the spirit standing in the corner of his jail cell said.

"As many times as I want to. Sometimes it's my only way out of this damn place." He quickly brought it down to a whisper, knowing he didn't want to add insanity to his record.

"You aren't happy with the justice they finally gave you?"

"I would've been happier with the millions I had stolen."

"Free one trial, guilty the next. And what about me?" the spirit asked.

"I didn't know a plaintiff had a concealed weapon and would miss me. I'm so sorry, Bro," he sobbed.

"If sorry, were a peanut butter sandwich…"

He walked through the palace halls knowing all too well his rivals would eventually discover the true nature of his crime. He might as well have been wearing his confession on his sleeve. The obvious was oozing out of the secret places. Just how many heads could he send rolling before the knives of the royals found his sinful heart?

"Sire? Oh, excuse me, Sire?" It was his jester motioning him to come down the hall to the library.

Other than the two guards posted at the ends of the long stone hallway, no one was in sight. He really didn't have time for this fool, but maybe he could get a good laugh, one he could certainly use right about now.

As his king entered the room, the jester, carrying his lute, bowed.

"You look worried, sire, and if not worried, weary."

"It's none of your concern, Jordan."

Strumming his lute, Jordan sang,

"Fear not the rabble; fear not the storm

For all have secrets from whence they're born

Tis the way of man to still his hand

Whenever heads roll throughout the land

We're all in darkness

We live in fright

Glad to keep our heads

From the fury and the might."

"Why thank you, I feel much better," said the king smiling, tossing his jester a coin.

The king strolled out into the courtyard. The jester called back to him.

He turned, arrows from the upper level rained down on him.

His queen stepped out from behind the curtain in the library. "Is he... ?"

"Yes, my lady," the jester said, receiving a coin.

She walked over to her dying king and knelt. "Death is better from one who loves you than from those you've feared."

He smiled as she closed his eyes.

XII

All I wanted was to live in peace. I never held any strong feelings of hate for anyone. While I held misgivings or misunderstandings as to why anyone would feel the need to destroy the lives of any group of people, I still made an effort to live in peace, until the day my wife and two daughters lost their lives in an airstrike.

Life would never be the same. There was no end to the suffering I was experiencing. I saw their faces, heard their voices, felt their hands in mine, and I remembered the laughter I so yearned to hear again, but would ever be denied. My children, my wife, this was not the life I had envisioned as a young man.

What a fool I was even to assume I could remain untouched. All of us now live under the shadow of this "Death from the West." So many families, so few survivors, and those committing these atrocities don't even realize the beast they've become. A creature that has claimed them as its own, for we are no longer just fighting them, but the Beast of War itself.

I am but one man with only one life to give, feeling if this is all I can sacrifice in the name of resistance, then so be it. They may kill me any time, at any moment, without even thinking twice about it. So if I must join my wife and daughters again, let me do so standing as a man, just to make the beast know my name is Resistance.

Death will find me breaking down its door!

After the allied soldier finished reading the last few pages of the diary, he mentioned it to his sergeant.

"Burn that piece of trash!" the sergeant ordered.

XIII

The United Nations in New York was holding its annual meeting, only to realize it wasn't the meeting they thought it would be. As the world's delegates gathered and took their seats, a column of darkness, extending from the floor to the ceiling, appeared in the area of the podium.

Guards attempted to draw their weapons only to find they couldn't. A voice spoke heard in the tongue of every attending delegate.

"We thank you for your assistance in bringing your planet to the brink of your self-induced annihilation." The voice was crude and rough, with a faint background echo. "We thought it would take you longer than most species, but not only have you surpassed others in your ignorance of the interdependence of all life on your planet, your tendencies for violence against each other, your planet, and other life forms are astounding, causing us to recalculate our timeline for 'Human Extermination.'"

The voice moved the delegates, it continued.

"There have been several near extinction of your species. I believe this will be the fifth and final curtain for your kind. After all, you are a selfishly driven species where your idea of tomorrow is to repeat the same atrocities committed today and yesterday as long as a sustain a profit. For you, being is taking; you attempt to clean your world with filthy and corrupted hands. Our fleet is far, but still close enough to be here upon your demise."

An arm jutted out from the column of darkness, three claws showing.

"Again, I salute you and your memory! Your replacement is already in progress."

The column of darkness was gone. Upon reviewing the security tapes, there was nothing, not even evidence of the passage of time. Many would come to believe the event, but not enough.

XIV

They had come too far, and there was no turning back. The family was beginning to lose faith. Their dream was crumbling down around them.

They thought traveling west would be the dream of a lifetime with the hope of finding gold, land, and prosperity "there for the taking."

Instead, rocks, dust, thirst, sore backsides, a desert heat that tore at their spirit, shredding apart their hopes and aspirations.

Two horses dead, livestock cut in half, and Ma was battling a fever she could no longer handle. Junior was looking at his father. Their eyes betrayed what to expect and what they would need to do.

They were worried about losing the trail, especially after a massive rainstorm washed out the road before entering the mountains. The wife and mother found her resting place at the foot of the mountains.

The father, son, and both daughters lost for words didn't speak. They buried her in her Sunday best and the violet scarf she always loved.

Their maps destroyed, still, every evening as the sun began to set, a light source from a lantern or something appeared in the distance far down the road ahead of them. Father felt the need to follow it as if somehow providence played a role in its appearance.

Weeks went by, but every evening he would move in the directions of the light.

Finally, they were free of the mountains: they found a badly beaten happiness and nurtured it back to life. When they neared a lake, Father undid the horses and walked to the lake to fill his canteen. There on a rock by the shoreline was the violet scarf of his wife. He collapsed to his knees, cried uncontrollably as did his children, realizing it was she who got them through.

XV

Duke and Becky were inseparable ever since he was a playful pup, and she a five-year-old tree-climbing girl. They would spend their days together in the woods, primarily when the weather was warm, and after ten years of being together, she knew better than to stay out after dark in the woods, unless it was an official camping trip.

It became darker than usual, nearing 8:30 pm and still no sign of them. Feeling a little anxious, the girl's father decided to sit out on the porch, keeping an eye out on the forest road leading up from the darkening woods.

Becky didn't come home that night, neither did Duke.

They notified the authorities. After an Amber Alert. Reporters and camerapersons found their way to their cabin. Just as Becky's dad was giving the police further details, up came Duke, barking and looking disheveled, he yelped as if motioning them to come, they quickly fell into pursuit. After a half an hour, they found Duke in a small clearing, jumping up and down frantically, looking toward the sky. They had a difficult time removing the big dog from the spot, but they couldn't see anything and were baffled by his behavior. They searched the area, but founding nothing, called off the search.

Her father took the agitated Duke home. Around the same time at night that she went missing, Duke, in heighten excitement, pushed the screen door open and took off barking.

Again those remaining followed in the darkness. Everyone spotted a glow in the distance. Duke's barking stopped, and he was gone.

They never found Becky and Duke. Three years later, her father tearfully packing her personals for storage, found her diary, and read on a bookmarked page the words, "Skyward, always skyward!"

XVI

The construction crew came across a burial site during their earth removal stage. The site manager told them to keep their mouths shut and not to disclose any information to anyone. Emphasizing anyone!

He couldn't afford a delay for money spoke louder than some damn bones.

He had the remains covered, got in his truck. He would deal with it in the morning. From his peripheral, he thought he caught a glimpse of someone standing to his side looking at him. He quickly turned, saw nothing.

That feeling of someone watching him would continue a few more times, at a gas station, a coffee shop, and the exit sign on his route home.

Upon arriving home, his family greeted him, his daughter saying, "Daddy, Daddy, we got the DNA report! See?" she said, handing it to him, "We are part Native American!"

"What?" he responded while taking off his jacket.

His wife added, "Yes, so it seems dear. Your ancestors were a part of an indigenous group living in this very region. The report indicates many got killed by government troops and then buried in a mass grave somewhere near here.

He sat down, reading the report.

"How could anyone kill a large number of people and just throw them in a pit, cover them up and erase them from history?" she asked.

"Wait, wait!" he raised his hand to calm her down and there it was again, that someone standing in his peripheral, he turned and saw the shape of a woman in native dress vanish.

In the morning, he called the state capital. He felt better informing them, but he felt humiliated knowing what he had done. To the end of his days, he would ask his ancestors for forgiveness.

XVII

Joe had forgotten what it was like after he came home from the war some forty years ago. He would suffer the tremors, the flashbacks, and the sickening feeling that they lied to him. He couldn't quite put his finger on it, but whenever he began to question the why of it all, the whole cycle and downward spiral would start all over again.

Displays of what the doctors felt was undesirable emotions lead to further medication.

Was he a man with independent thoughts or a sponge?

His country turned him into a killing machine only to anesthetize him for the rest of his life.

He knew how he felt, some of his comrades became more family than family, more than blood, and to watch or hear them die never entirely justified his reasoning for participating in the killing of innocents. His grief, no longer distant, walked with him, stared him in the mirror, laid with him, loved him. They would never understand because he still couldn't understand.

It wasn't about coming back home to fulfill that American dream. The government dehumanized Joe: but he beat the odds—this Vet survived. Now they just needed him to sleep, whether it's standing, sitting, eating or living. Be it drugs illegal, drugs official, TV, or finally surrendering to suicide—stop thinking, stop questioning was the order of the day.

Camped out on a corner in tattered civvies begging for a meal, and as a few coins hit his cup, he realized that his role was well-thought-out long ago in the original blueprint of making a soldier. Everyone is just doing their duty, even those who lie.

Life for him, after all, was no longer to be enjoyed. It was to be tolerated, for him and every warrior of his kind.

XVIII

The elders came together and chose Muata to begin as an initiate under Baba Koni, the village shaman.

He felt honored to learn from Baba Koni. But, there was more involved than he could ever imagine, some knowledge of husbandry, herbalism, elixirs, and infusions as well as the songs and poems that accompanied them. Muata was at a loss whenever Baba Koni would ask him to retrieve something from out of his hut. It was like finding a sand pebble in a mound of rocks.

Months passed when Baba Koni asked Muata to get a group of kola nuts in his hut as he needed to do a reading for a client. Without being disrespectful, Muata said, "Baba, it is hard to find the items you ask me to find. I am lost whenever I enter your abode. I'm sorry, but if your life is anything like your hut, then your life is a mess!"

"Mande, good!" his Baba rejoiced. "Today, you have completed your first lesson!"

Muata looked confused.

"Lesson one," Baba Koni smiled at him, "Life is a mess!"

"What?" asked Muata.

Chaos is in all things. When you become the gifted shaman I believe you to be; then your role will be to help others 'walk-in balance' within the realm of life's chaos or as you say 'Mess.'" He got up and went over to collect two brooms, but continued, "Balance is key to everything, be it body, mind or spirit, health, relationships or beliefs. Too much of anything, and one can become off-balance."

Muata finally understood. Just then, Baba shoved one of the brooms in his hand. "Forget the kola nuts; let's go balance out my mess." He and Muata had a good laugh. Muata would enjoy the company of his mentor.

XIX

Considering the amount of training that had gone into preparing them for the event they were now facing, they were still unprepared. The astronauts were operating an Earth vessel Meteor Impact 12 from an orbiting platform station.

Twenty-six years earlier, Earth's moon was nearly blown in half by what appeared to have been an enormous meteor slamming into the dark side of the moon, leaving billions of bits of moon and meteor debris that had formed an unstable ring around the planet.

Forty-eight Meteor Impact vessels had been deployed to police the near-earth space against any unstable debris large enough to cause considerable damage to any populated areas and push the debris away from Earth. Scientists estimated that it could take a few thousand years before Earth's ring became stabilized. Of course, there was always the remaining fear that other outside meteors could still cause a cascade effect and trigger unknown catastrophic events.

Many small and unseen fragments pelted the orbiting platform, that communication with Meteor Impact 12 became garbled, sending it into a route ahead of a meteor chunk instead of into it. It acted as a shield protecting the meteor from being burned up in Earth's atmosphere. The meteorite was as giant as a decent size house.

Ground missiles honed in but destroyed Meteor Impact 12 instead. The government implemented Evacuation protocols, but as always, they fell short of being useful as only a few would escape given the time frame and proximity to Earth. The meteor came in at a scrapping angle, wiping out a considerable portion of the eastern United States coastline, leaving an untold number of casualties.

Earthlings had a new fear to face, a new threat added to the roster of disasters facing them every day.

XX

The artist wasn't real, just a copy, a look-a-like version made to make the rest of us feel that little to nothing had changed, that the continuity would or could refill the emptiness that came into being when we lost our idol.

Still, most of the audience enjoyed the antics, the gestures, the mimics, body language, and twerks. The performer was close enough to rekindle the fire some felt for their once-beloved idol. Still, for a few others in the auditorium, that performer was just an echo reminding them of the praise, honor, and attention they should've given their living genius, possibly causing them to look at themselves in relation to the artists still living amongst them.

However, getting too deep in thought about the subject would be an injustice to the current entertainer doing their best on the stage. Shaking that feeling that this was all a fake was still too hard to dismiss. The great-sounding music was just loud enough to cover-up any missed cues or off-notes and kept the crowd jumping.

The show would go on, reaching the climax that the original artist would have reached, leaving you to wonder if the spirit of the artist was watching this circus. What did they feel about it? Would it be a humble thank you or roaring laughter because the spirit wasn't there and that was the one thing that was certain about it? The artist wasn't there, just an impersonation of the spirit.*

*Story idea from my wife after a concert we attended.

XXI

"Explain me to the committee; just who do they think they are? They couldn't smell genius if they rubbed their noses in it.

"It was I who made this company the giant it is today, and now they demand I go before the board and explain my new project? Idiots!"

He slammed down the phone in his office and went over to click the hidden wall panel to enter his secret lab. Roger, his assistant, was finishing the project as planned.

"Almost finished, sir," Roger said.

"What's taking you so damn long? You should have finished this morning, you moron! God, why do I surround myself with such mindless apes?" He pushed Roger out of his way as he went over to inspect his "Actual-Livebot," AL 13. "The board is trying to steal my project; I know how those greedy bastards think. Suit me up, and let's do this."

"Are you sure?"

"Do as I tell you, you fool!"

Roger didn't care for him much, but he did as he followed orders, wiring Dr. Hodges up for cerebral-engram transplantation, placing his mind/memories into a superior, long-life automaton. After the successful transfer, Roger clubbed the lifeless body of Dr. Hodges, just as the AL 13 was rising from the table. He grabbed the body, dragged it out into the hallway, told security that the robot had broken one of the moral laws, and killed a human. "Restrain it, restrain it; it's gone mad."

Dr. Hodges tried to speak from his AL 13 but found his speech mechanism dismantled. Guards placed hand and leg restraints on the AL 13. Dr. Hodges realized what Roger had done when he saw Roger, with a knowing smile on his face, holding his body.

"Place it in 100-year storage," ordered a board member.

XXII

The day was still gray, somewhat mild, not as chilly as the day before, but again, a signature type of day considering the season was coming to a close. It would be getting colder soon, making yesterday's chill seem quite balmy by comparison. I noticed the relaxing, asphalt road swerving down toward the coastline away from the wooded area, and I could see the sea rhythmically grasping at a short piece of sandy beach off to my left. Out there somewhere over the sea, sunlight was breaking through the clouds in hard and soft beams of light. I remember wishing somehow that light could eventually reach me.

There was room to pull over and take in the scenery. I was always rushing, always dismissing my surroundings. Not today, not now. I needed this. The smell of the salty sea and forest pine mixed in with the soft breeze that wrapped around my vehicle and flowed through the open window. I got out and stood there, searching for feelings long gone. Still, there was that itch.

The world was different now; its flavor had changed. I didn't have much time: in fact, I was taking a significant risk just being on the road at this time of day. I turned around and reached for the scope of my sniper rifle.

I detached the scope and cautiously scanned my surroundings. It was a precautionary measure that I'd become accustomed to doing. My nemesis was there below me, coming up the winding path. I grabbed my rifle, slid on the scope, focused, fired three quick shots, and then I saw his car careen over the cliff. I put the gun away, climbed back in my car, took in one more whiff of the salty breeze, smiled, and drove on to my next kill.

XXIII

There was little to no agreement when the orders came in for retreat. A few of the less experienced officers felt there was enough of a slim chance that the battle could be taken, at least from their viewpoint. However, the field commander expressed a concern that there would need to be a realignment of their forces. Also, he wanted the enemy to start believing they might have the upper hand by having his forces withdraw to a critical point.

They argued about the orders, some cursing under the thunder of the battle; still, they followed them. They retreated some 400 meters to find a new unit of fresh troops dug in and ready. Sure enough, the enemy took the bait and was quickly in pursuit, thinning out their forces as they charged.

The commander's forces realigned themselves with the fresh troops, the reorganizing of their strengths offered a more definitive victory than the mere possibility of one that had existed earlier. Many of the younger, novice recruits began to appreciate the wisdom and experience of their commander and how a sacrifice in some areas of conflict could eventually lead to a favorable outcome in the long run.

XXIV

He'd lie on his bunk against the dark gray wall of his cell and start thinking how he didn't want to be part of his gang anymore. Still, they were family, and they had been there for him as he had been for them. That vibrantly charged feeling of living dangerously on edge—like a hard game of tag where the "tags" were permanent, worthy of recognition. Folks let you know where you stood with them, no bull shit.

Manny had taken the fall by saying that the gun used in the killing was his. He was finishing up a hard seven years.

Now that he was reeling in his last days, he questioned his role with his crew; he wanted another direction for them but knew about their fear of change. In prison, he had plenty of time to think about his path, all 360 degrees of it.

He had grown into somewhat of a realist. He knew of the limits his society would place on him, but more importantly, he began to understand the restrictions he put and was still putting on himself.

Youth, with all its drive and ignorance, seemed to be unending, always in front of him. However, here he met old-timers, players from the schoolyard of life before his time. He didn't want to settle where they settled or face their resolve.

He needed specific answers to questions he knew his crew never asked.

When released, he could taste his chances, and there was nothing sweet in the taste. He never told his "family" his release date. With his gate money, he would take the bus in the opposite direction. He'd meet up with his parole officer later. He just needed time, hopefully, more time than they gave him.

XXV

One of the gods walked into the temple hall where the other gods were convening, took off his headgear, undid his robe, and threw up his hands, "Man! Man! Why did we ever consider making those fools? They're always asking for something. Can I please have a little bit of this or a little bit that?"

He walked over to the other side of the temple, sat down in a huff, and scratched his head with frustrated hands.

"What do they want this time?" asked his wife as she came over to massage his shoulders. "Lord, aren't you stressed!"

"One country is sending up prayers and sacrifices to me, asking that I be on their side in an up and coming war, and their enemy is doing the very same thing. Don't they understand there is no God of War? I'm just me, a nice deity, who wants everybody just to get along!"

"You know?" a voice came from a goddess, at the other end of the temple, raising her hand. "We can always make a God of War." The other gods laughed in a momentary thunder. "No, wait, I'm serious, he or she doesn't have to be anything special. I mean, if your wife wouldn't mind you and me having a little roll in the clouds," she said, looking playfully at the both of them.

The other gods quietly rumbled.

"Okay," his wife allowed, "but nothing too powerful."

Her husband went off with the goddess and, after a little turbulence in the clouds; they came back with a small infant boy.

There was applause throughout the temple halls.

Who knew then that the little tyke would grow up to be the most popular deity of them all?

XXVI

"The machine needs cogs. They don't have to be happy, and they certainly don't have to think for themselves. Whatever dreams they are allowed to dream, we will provide them," the corporate leader spoke to the board members at the annual meeting. "Our role is not to give them hope but to offer its fragrance, its allure. We'll pay them enough, make them want enough, to spend enough, to keep them in the state they currently reside.

"There are some of you here tonight, fortunately only a few who believe that wealth is something to share. Well, let me correct you. For now and in the future, wealth is something to cherish. We accumulate it, to build upon and, with enough foresight, control those we need to control. Let's face it, meager and humbling as many of the masses may seem; they are no better than rats scurrying through life with no plans, only an appetite for chaos.

"They would eat themselves if they could. Consume, which is why we relegate the bastards to the sub-status of a consumer. When the fortunate few come into 'wealth,' all they do is buy as directed by the dreams and aspirations we have given them over the decades. They spend, spend, and spend, collecting the frivolous, the meaningless.

"Your only concern is to ensure they never truly learn the strength that comes from supporting one another, creating any viable system that would enhance their love or respect for each other. For the moment, should any of them learn to invest in themselves and begin seeing what a true commodity each could afford the other, the corrosion of our control would begin, ending our way of life! To maintain the system!"

They rose from their seats, applauded, and waited for the next speaker.

XXVII

In the old days, the neighborhood felt like a living organism, with eyes, ears, mouth, and some would argue even a stomach considering the hunger it always felt. For sure, it would always squeal to our mama or papa should we act out of line.

Some days we could feel it breathing, the flashing colors, and the glare of sunlight bouncing off concrete and the tops of large sedans with chrome that bragged their status and offered a history of the "what-we-got" of some families.

Streets seemed cleaner back then; maybe it was a personal thing, more our block and their block—a matter of pride. Gangs named themselves after the streets where they lived.

Drums simmered in the summer; snowball fights flurried in the winter on mounds of snow left by bulldozers on either side of the avenue. We'd turn them into forts using aerial bombardments of snowballs onto the other hill; we'd play 'til our toes froze.

We never used building addresses to go from place to place; instead, we ran basements, using them as a tunneling system, jumping walls lined with sharp glass shards, dodging the anger of supers who would love to skin our hides should they ever got their hands on us.

I spent a lot of time in the park watching the elders playing checkers, chess, and listening to their stories, and the hollow threats shouted in a heated game of horseshoes.

The neighborhood was a refuge, a cocoon where so many of us young cats (caterpillars) lovingly molted into who we are. Of course, once we got our wings, life would never be the same.

XXVIII

The spider queen lowered herself down from the upper branches to visit her family members and came across Little Sister.

"Little Sis, why such a big web?" she asked.

Staying busy with her web building, she answered, "Because the prey I seek is big and juicy, delicious to the taste and can last a long, long time. I hear it can be passed around and around to many, but it's hard to catch, yet easy to accept. I really don't know what that means, and I have yet to see what one looks like, but I hear it can grow enormous and I'm certain if I build a big enough and strong enough web, I'll be able to catch it, and I'll never have to go hungry again."

"And what exactly is this prey called?" the spider queen asked, having grown curious.

"I heard it's called a 'LIE.'"

"You mean 'FLY' of course. I know you've always had a difficult time pronouncing your 'F's. But it's called a FLY!"

"No, it's called a 'LIE' and from what I hear they're everywhere, billions of them. And anyway I've mastered the 'F' sound, and I know what a FLY is, so there!" she replied, sticking out her tongue.

Spider queen looked at her younger sister; if she had eyebrows, she would've knitted all eight of them. She turned to go back up to her web, quietly laughing to herself and said, "Believe me, honey child, stick to flies!"

She had had enough of the family for one day.

XXIX

He couldn't keep his hands off the relic, an ancient amulet from centuries-long passed. He was drawn to it and got an incredible sense of well-being from it. He could occasionally put it down, but liken it to the opium dens he used to visit as a young man. He would need to pick it up and sit with it for a spell. However, after a while, the effects wore off, and nightmarish visions began to accompany the handling of the relic. From glances at the mirror, he noticed he had aged at least a good ten years.

He called his friend, who was a doctor, to examine him. For some reason, there was a strong urge to rid himself of the amulet. He shared it with his doctor. Upon allowing the doctor to handle it, the doctor got an immediate aroused mental state. He wanted to hold on to the piece, looking at the amulet and scrutinizing it.

"What's this patch of skin on the back? Why is it shaped like a heart!"

"Animal skin probably, it's in the crafting of some of those ancient relics back then."

"This is not animal skin; this is human skin. Let's give you that checkup. I want to hold on to this." the doctor said, wanting it for himself. However, after a while, it would be shared with another poor soul.

On the other side of the world, there was a young man who stayed young as if his life force constantly renewed itself or sucked from the lives of others. He lived centuries, changing locale whenever necessary. When asked how he was able to stay looking so young, he'd answer, "Why it comes from sharing; it's good for the heart."

Grinning as he rubbed the heart-shaped scar on his chest.

XXX

"Fear has become so real, that life has become unnatural," Edgar said to himself, turning off the TV. He didn't want to hear about another killing of one more young black man by police. He sat in his chair; lowered the room lights while peeking through the blinds out onto the dark street.

'They're looking to pull the trigger; they're on automatic whenever they see us. Police incapable of dismissing the images programmed into them since conception. They see only the images, not the man, the woman, or the child. They see us as a 'justifiable threat' that they've come to expect when confronting us. We've come to understand how they see us; it's now the way we see ourselves as well. We know they can kill us and face virtually no consequence; it's become a 'right,' a 'free pass,' leaving us to fear them even more. Two fears provoking each other, and, with one wrong misstep, a life is lost, usually ours," he mumbled.

Edgar continued to peer down the avenue. He saw the first group of them approaching; they were the spawn of fear—Hate. Shadowy creatures were traveling in packs, some on streets, some moving through the air, sniffing always sniffing, looking for open doors, for people quarreling, for openings, for an opportunity.

"Some people see spirits. Why do I have to see emotions?"

Edgar started beating his fist against his head, seeing them at all times of the day. But night, God the night! The question came to him; did we possibly make these monsters? He thought about taking his medication, and then he remembered love's beauty. No, I need to see them, a reminder of the fear and hate in this world. He slowly closed the blinds, "I'll wait, maybe Love will return someday."

XXXI

"Can you be certain, are you sure?"

"What more proof do you want?" cried his grandson, throwing his brother's blood-stained spear at his grandfather's feet.

"He killed your brother, my father, and his brother and now has killed my brother. I barely got away with my life. Why does Dark Shadow hate us so and target our family when he comes to our region? He is only an elephant?"

His grandfather bent over and picked up his dead grandson's spear and held it in hands, tears flowing down his worn, leathered face. "He hasn't forgotten. I suppose he'll hate us until his dying day."

"Hate us? What are you talking about, grandfather?"

His grandfather motioned to him to assist him in getting up and guided him to a wall where he took down two carved tusks. He gathered them in his arms, caressing them as if he weaved his memory was into them. "Here, take these." His grandson looked at him strangely.

He understood the gaze staring back at him, "Your granduncle and I killed an elephant in our youth. Little did we realize she was Dark Shadow's mate! He wasn't even in the area, yet somehow he knew and taken revenge ever since."

He touched his grandson's face, "Enough blood lost, enough memories lost. Tomorrow take these to the site where he killed your brother and offer them to Dark Shadow. Be careful!"

The rising sun found his grandson at the site. Dark Shadow was not far away, and upon seeing him, he took a charging stance. Quickly, but gently he unwrapped the two tusks and set them down, humbly backing off.

Dark Shadow moved in to pick up the two tusks, held them, and let out a roar. The young man knew it was for a lost love.

XXXII

The line of men was getting thinner; still, they were marching up the path. They would eventually reach the fortress.

A blizzard raged, and the soldiers on the ramparts couldn't get a clear view of those drawing ever so near. The one thing they were able to recognize was the enemy's colors the men wore. With that in mind, a volley of arrows, spears, rocks, and boiling oil went over the walls.

"I think I see one of them holding a flag of truce," cried a soldier along the battlement.

"To hell with those bastards, I don't want a truce. I want them dead!" the commander yelled. "They killed my brother; let there be nothing left of them."

In the morning, the snowstorm had dissipated. The commander and an armed group of warriors went outside the gate to check on the remains. Instead of finding enemy troops, they discovered their men, apparently captured and released, only dressed in the colors of their enemy. The warrior holding the flag of truce was his brother.

The commander knelt over him: he didn't know what to say; after all, it was his order to refuse a truce that had his brother killed. "I'm sorry, brother. It appears we no longer kill our enemy, but anyone in the image of our enemy. Has our hate grown so deep and dark?"

He stood up and saluted his brother and the other dead around him. He called for the burial detail. Maybe, he thought, just maybe this would be an excellent time to consider a truce and ultimate peace. He had his doubts; still, he would seek an audience with the Crown Prince.

XXXIII

Sitting quietly on the mountainside, along the edge of the forest clearing, he looked at the newly erected fort down in the distance. He understood little about the culture of the invaders. However, he realized this fort meant the expansion of their people and the ending of his own.

First was the conversion, taking the beliefs that had kept us living in harmony far longer than memory itself, sure we had disputes, but nothing like this. They tell us our way is evil and their way true. I see it only as a belief they teach but don't follow.

They flood our land with words on paper, only to take our area, calling it their own. They send out few to bring in many, appearing humble only to bite with hidden fangs, leaving us poisoned and confused. And now because they can take, they take, because their nation can kill many, they kill many.

They seduce, charm, and lie, saying all is good between us when good means how much they've gained and how much we've lost.

And so now stands their fort against the blue sky and plains of living colors. Surely justice will not abide there for us, only for them, for them, it means "just us."

He watched the gate open, and four riders head out toward him. They come for me, policing the area as they always do. Maybe they will take this life as the lives of so many of my people, but not today. He mounted his horse and rode.

XXXIV

They would never understand her solitude; her need to be alone. Everyone had plans for her life. They were life constructionists, life choreographers, and life-interior designers. They dug the paths, built the sets, wrote the dance numbers, and placed the curtains in every room of her life.

She never felt the need for inclusion, but others would continually push and pull. Too meek to contradict or go against their assumptions of what would be right or best for her or who would be right or best for her, she would just take it all in.

They never accepted her wishes because they never honestly asked her, and for those who did, her wants were too simple for such a pretty young lady like herself. From all the mounting pressure to be someone or something she never wanted, she had a major breakdown at twenty-seven years of age, resulting in suicide.

Society builds the mold and goes out of its way to make sure everyone fits it as close as possible, and if you don't have the strength to break the mold, the mold will break you. There's peace through conformity, to look alike, act alike, and think alike.

The ringleaders, the lion tamers, all denounced their manipulation and involvement by saying, "We always knew she was unstable!"

They gathered in their little groups, their small social circles, the constructionists, the choreographers and the interior designers, exchanging notes, rumors, and preprogrammed opinions. After a period, they all rose like gears in a clock. They sanitized any semblance of guilt and moved on to the next child.

XXXV

In the beginning, begging was tough, an embarrassment for me, as it went against my social and formative upbringing. But after dealing with failure, after failure, after countless failures, I've come to realize a truth about me, I have a low threshold. Begging may be something I happen to do reasonably well. I was never encouraged to see failure as a starting point, an opportunity to begin at something new or different.

Failure meant humiliation, public or private, plain, and simple. It was what my father taught me, his father taught him, and what I came to believe. Now I've reached a point where I tried my best to avoid mirrors, anything that would cast my reflection revealing or reminding me of the height from which I've fallen. The least I can do is avoid looking at myself, who knows if I can't see me then maybe the rest of the world can't see and won't see me as a failure. I could, and I think I can, in fact, become invisible. Hidden from the world, like the favorite childhood game we use to play, "Hide and Go Seek," yeah, "Hide and Go Seek" and like then as like it is today, no one would seek me out, no one paid attention as to whether I anyone found me or not.

Still, as much as I would love to vanish, every now and then there is that itch to connect—begging allows me that temporary magical portal where only the caring can see me, the rest will go on ignoring me with disgust or contempt. Does it matter, though? I know a day will come when I will achieve invisibility, or will I be a failure at that too? Now, if only I could laugh at myself.

The Elderly Care Act, a bill that would set an extermination age for the elderly, introduced to Congress for the third time in thirteen years.

It failed twice before because it included all elders. Both houses fought to introduce an exclusionary clause that would exclude distinct members in specific areas of government, corporate, and religious sectors to be due to their "experience." In other words, the elders in those areas wanted to avoid extermination.

Again as in the past, the world rose against the concept, with worldwide protest, sabotage, and terrorist acts. The media and press, as always, played their roles accordingly.

Senator Singleton of Maine was the first of several whistleblowers to take a stand and inform the American public of the truth behind the Elderly Care Act, speaking from a French news station.

"Do not believe this charade, this red flag, this Elderly Care Act. The killing of hundreds of thousands of citizens from every walk of life has been part of this government's plan for decades. They will have you believe they're targeting a specific group. I have data, proof, documented evidence our government has been conspiring with corporate leaders to exterminate a calculated number of our citizens each year, ensuring its quota, by any means necessary!

"These records indicate an unwillingness to release real cures, pertinent info revealing the poisoning of air and water, cancer, smoking, drugs, opioids, healthcare. The government's refusal to set gun control legislation, our vaccines, GMOs, poverty, crime, and prison system, and our wars are all signs of their willingness to adhere to the plan. See you in D.C."

This report just in—"Libyan terrorist bombs flight 230—Paris to Washington, killing all 139 passengers, a young senator from Maine believed to be among them."

XXXVII

"You don't need a teacher to pass out facts and info; anyone can do that. You need a teacher to reveal to students a path of discovery, not only of the world outside but the world inside.

"To be in awe of the 'can do' and the 'can be' of their possibilities. A teacher nurtures the vehicle of their expression, that body part that they will sing their life's song through. Will they show magic through their hands, voice, physique, or their mind? I try to discover in them the steed that will carry them through their life, bringing them peace, joy, happiness—not the desire to be among the top-ten on someone's chart or statistic sheet. Not every flower blossoms in the same way or at the same time; let them play at learning.

"You grade them based on how close they are to reaching your goal, not on how close they are to reaching theirs. At least give students a yearning to learn."

"You're very poetic in your approach, professor, but what would be their goal?"

"I don't know."

"Exactly our point!"

"You don't need to know their goal: all you have to do is teach them the love of learning."

"But then we wouldn't control the outcome; they would be free to think and do for themselves."

"Yes, I understand your need to control them by giving them the illusion they are free, when in reality should they love learning, they'll discover the lies you teach and what happens then?"

"I'm sorry, professor: the board has decided you are not qualified to teach at our institution, and you will be blacklisted should you attempt to teach elsewhere."

The professor finally found a village in a place in the world where the love for learning would blossom.

XXXVIII

Midday found us standing near the corner underneath the shade of a decent-size oak. The hot season was upon us, and a good few of us hadn't been out since winter. But now, with the heat and a lot less clothing worn by the hotties, we needed to be there for roll call.

Like the pigeons that gathered beneath the EL train, squawking with the sunrise to let every other pigeon know who was there, we would assemble offering deep hugs, complicated handshakes, and a variety of high and low fives, our "ritual of survivors." After the initial greetings, a fast flood of stories came. Rumors full of a who's who, of those who passed; those hospitalized. Tidbits on those vacationing in jail, and those who needed some fast and hard favors—like cash.

Sometimes we'd let a few newcomers join our old flock. We welcomed them, just not always trusted them until the friendship hardened. We'd set up our teams, some to the hospital, others sending cards and letters to those on "vacation," and some passing out extra bucks if we could spare any. Mostly, it would be little to none.

Sometimes the laughter that would shake the corner turned into ugly, unnecessary squabbles. But, like clockwork, a sweet ass would pass by, and our one-track minds went back onto that one track.

It was a yearly gathering, a roll call we felt we needed to attend, knowing that next summer, anyone of us could be part of the conversation, "Did you hear so-and-so passed?"

Too old to chase the skirts we longed for, but not too old to look, we would just resonate with the vibe of just being alive. Our one hope would be to be there at next summer's roll call.

XXXIX

"Your problem is you don't think we think. You come here, flaunting your arrogance, and you're better than thou attitude and expect the rest of the world to bow at your feet, thinking, 'God, we finally got the chance to be blessed by your presence.'

"Your self-righteous refusal to be open to other ideas, other concepts and customs, and other ways of life is astounding. The possession of wealth and ownership of intelligence are entirely different things. You can't discover lands already occupied by people: but to hear you tell it, you discovered the world! Get over yourselves!

"You master the art of killing people in mass numbers, and you think yourself smarter than everyone else. You know more about killing then you do about living. Death is the trophy you hang on your walls.

"You come to understand the nature of a thing by destroying it, breaking it down, finding its weakness—an approach you use on men, women, and children, and every other form of life. You make me sick to my stomach!"

Upon hearing the house bell ring, 54-year-old Kabir pulled himself and his rant away from the bathroom mirror. Fixed his turban, his collar, collected himself, and came out toward the kitchen.

He could hear the British commandant yelling from outside, "Boy? Boy! Where the hell is that tea? Damn these people!"

"Yes Sahib, I am coming, I am coming."

He grabbed the tea tray, cloth napkins, and quickly but orderly rushed out to the patio, apologizing to the commandant and his guests for his tardiness.

The elder walked through the center of his village, smiling as he watched groups of children playing. They played different games according to their age groups, as was common when he was a child. He came upon a group of children circling a child they had humiliated. She sang back at them a new rhyme he never heard, "Sticks and stones may break my bones, but words will never hurt me."

He threw down his staff, went over, and grabbed the girl's arm, demanding to know whose child she was.

Naturally, everyone in the village came over to see what could make their gentle Baba Sekou so upset.

When her parents came, he wanted to know who taught her that song, telling the child to repeat it.

"Oh, that's just something they learned at the missionary school," her mother calmly explained.

"Sit! Everybody sit and hand me, my staff."

Out of respect, they all knelt.

"Such lies, such lies. Words are more powerful than sticks and stones." They looked surprised.

"Tell me, what is a word? I asked you what is a word?"

"Just a word?" someone meekly answered.

"No, a word is how we see the 'Egulu,' the invisible creatures of the mind. If I say drum, you see drum; if I say sandal, you see sandal. But words like stupid, ugly, or worse—well those are Egulu clinging, choking and suffocating you for the rest of your life. Broken bones can heal, but none of us can see the harmful Egulu attached to our brothers or sisters. There are Egulu who strengthen you like love, smart, brave, beautiful. Thoughts are living creatures: words are how we see them. There is more to this life then what their schools will ever teach you.

"Now, go play." He smiled.

Matthews had holstered his gun having killed two beloved homesteaders who moved on land his cattle used for grazing. He quickly grabbed a few of their personal effects. He knew just the guy to pin the evidence on, that new gambler who just came into town and won a lot of Matthews' money at the saloon last Saturday night.

The town's people were up in arms when news of the deaths of the Williams reached town. Rumors, started by friends of Matthews, suggested someone check the rooms of any newcomers. The Sheriff and his deputies found personal possessions belonging to the Williams in the gambler's saddlebag in his hotel room.

They went over to the gambling saloon and arrested Mr. Samuels, who was sitting at the table with a winning hand.

A mob appeared screaming to string Samuels up. The trial was quick, setting a date for the hanging == tomorrow.

That night before the hanging, Samuels was finally able to secure his time-traveling device from the jammed heel of his boot. "I didn't take a vacation from the future only to die here in the past!" he said, pressing the button and returning to the future.

A deputy passing the cell, and seeing it empty, rushed to the front to tell the Sheriff that Samuels was gone.

"What the hell!" he screamed, grabbing his deputy by the collar, "We got a hanging tomorrow and damn it, we're gonna hang somebody. You and the boys find someone. Justice will be served!"

Looking around, they found Matthews alone, drunk as a skunk, satisfied that his plan worked out. They brought him to the Sheriff.

"He'll do. He's the right size."

They gagged him, hooded his head, and marched him out to the gallows in the morning. The people got their justice.

XLII

The morning dew caught him by surprise. He was, after all, a city boy where concrete was his grass, brick, and mortar his tree bark and skyscrapers his mountain range.

There was a sweet, heavy odor of chlorophyll, petals, and forest pine that bound him to the Earth in a manner unknown to him. The sound of a nearby babbling brook sparkled in comparison to the loud, charged noise of traffic that would keep him on his toes night and day.

The sky faded gradually from the stars of the night before into the dawning of the rising sun peeking over the distant mountains, radiating passed the silhouette of birds riding a strong wind in the distance. Even though summer was upon him, a chill would dance under the shade of every passing cloud.

Finally, a smile was given birth from his sometimes hardline, stone-chiseled face.

"Yes," he said, "Yes, they buried me in a good place!"

XLIII

The neighborhood had a warmth seasoned with flavors, colors, textures, and people from all over. The syncopated music from all over would snap and crackle like glass beads on a cheap neckpiece. But its bass would hover about six inches off the steamy, hot concrete pavement and your stride, your entire gait was genetically programmed to meet the beat.

The slang songs in every mother's tongue, out of every shop vendor and dealer who would three-card monte you into believing luck was "natural," and all you had to do was sing that note, play that tune or hit that number.

The nod, the sway, the rhythmic rumble of a sweet ass that made you forget the rent was due, or your electricity was about to be cut off by the Ed the Con man.

The spice was always there, whether or not your taste buds were in high gear or your ride had a flat. There were stoop-cooked-up recipes, from boy-girl sweet talk to stiletto sharp curses that cut and sliced in every direction, so you had to have your ninja shoes on mode "ready" just to duck those quacks.

Everyone's body, mind, and spirit owned something of and owed something to the music, the dance, the melodramatic refrain that christened our neighborhood "the Street."

But it all went soulfully silent the day a "drive-by" took the life of one of ours—a child, the seed of our song. That sweet, sweet child and now the flavor of our lives would never taste the same.

XLIV

The team of archaeologists had been searching for a hidden temple in the Amazonian jungle for what seemed ages, and their sponsors were tired of receiving little more than trinkets among the findings and reports sent back to the home office. They received word that their funding would end should no substantial reports arrive in the next few weeks.

The consuming heat, bothersome insects, and dangerous environment were harsh enough on them, only to have this news adding to the level of despair and doubt that lingered at the campsite. There was one last clue they would follow, one final area they needed to investigate.

They entered an area of jungle where their radio communication went dead. But, sure enough, deeper into the bush, they found a stone slab entrance. They were able to open it and enter into what appeared to be a still operational control center of some type with flashing electronic circuitry and with sophisticated, crystalline formations.

The team stood transfixed, questions avalanched one after another.

One of them walked over to a type of control panel.

"Touch nothing," one screamed, but it was too late; there was a deep low, earsplitting hum.

When they recovered, a viewing screen was activated showing a binary star system, they could see, from the ruins, this world was dead.

"How do we get back?" They tried reading the hieroglyphs.

"Don't know. I'll try again!"

With six attempts, they reached six destroyed worlds.

"It keeps showing only destroyed civilizations; wait here are a few yet to be x'ed out, third from its star. Try it."

They were back on Earth, but far from their sanity. They buried the entrance.

"You know what it means being on that list?" one said.

"I know…nothing…because we saw nothing. Agreed?"

They all agreed.

XLV

Reclining in her hospital bed, watching the rain of a dark, gray day drench the city she had come to love so well, she would play in her mind with the fluid, mosaic sequence of changing patterns of the view, created by the raindrops beating against her window pane.

Barely touching her food, she pushed the tray away, just as friends and relatives came in to visit. There was a small parade of grandchildren with cards and flowers and others who heard from the community grapevine that she took ill. She was overwhelmed by some of those who showed up: she hadn't seen them in years.

She would lie in her bed at night going over the day's guest list in her mind, wondering why some people wait until you're at death's door before they even think about coming to see you. The rain had moved on, and the lights of the newly washed cityscape sparkled like stars.

She did her best to go over some of the conversations with siblings, children, and grandchildren, chuckling at some of the darnedest things they'd say at their young age.

"Ah," she sighed, "I've been blessed." She then noticed the TV monitor was still on, playing another episode of that show "Law and something or other"—she reached for the controls to turn it off when the door to her room seemed to open with another group of folks, there was a light behind them.

"Visiting hours are over," she said, she was tired.

Still, they came in; her mother, her father, and her husband. She could feel her heart's joy at seeing their faces.

"Yes, dear," her husband said, taking her hand and kissing her, "Visiting hours are over."

XLVI

"So you've wasted a good part of your life hating, angry at everyone and everything, finding every justifiable reason or excuse to prove your superiority and their inferiority."

"It's time well spent," the 76-year-old man snarled at his granddaughter."

"How?" she asked.

"Because they are inferior, it's the Lord's truth, and there's no way you can persuade me to think otherwise!"

"Well, if they are inferior, then why spend so much time trying to prove it?"

"What do you mean?"

"Well, let's say," pointing to the family dog, "I would never have to worry about Spot taking my job, right? I mean he's just a dog, and it's a foregone conclusion he will never learn how to do computer programming. So I don't spend time proving it and I won't. I'm at ease."

"So what?"

"You can't hate the inferior if they're truly inferior, according to your way of thinking. Truthfully, there are people all over the world who are just as equal but simply look or think differently from you. Rather than appreciate the strength of diversity and the gifts others have to offer, you would suppress a world, always finding a reason or a lie to make you feel better or superior because, in truth, what you fear may be your inferiority."

"What the hell?" slamming his fist down, startling her. "If I didn't love you so much, I'd whip your hide!"

"I'm sorry, Gramps, but your hate comes from your fear! What do you fear?"

"I fear nothing!" he insisted.

"Then, before I leave for my new job on the West Coast, did you know my dad's father was black?"

"No!"

"Do you still love me now? I love you, Gramps!" She walked to her car, leaving him with his hate.

XLVII

"Time and space can record events," the castle tour guide explained to the curious group of seventeen onlookers. Dressed in early 13th-century garb, he would guide them through the halls and passageways of an old but famous haunted castle.

"Just because you walketh through air, like it haveth no source or substance, dost being in all virtue nothing, whereas fish moveth through water in fashion thus the same, there is still more to the understanding of the skies above and earth below than thou hast dreamt of."

"He means the world is stranger than you can imagine," whispered an elderly tourist to his son.

"Dad, I know what he means, but I wish he'd cut the crap with using that archaic bull." His son whispered in his ear.

"I say this to tell you," the guide continued, "My mentors believeth that a haunting tis the way this universe remembers exceptional, emotional events. So if any of you thus see a token or wisp of a spirit, still be thy heart. Thou looketh upon a memory."

He guided them to some of the castle's most popular haunting sites where recorded hauntings were known to occur.

They went through the castle catching mere glimpses of shifts in light or faint patterns appearing on the dab, stone walls. They couldn't say if what they saw were ghosts or if it was their imagination playing tricks on them.

At the end of the hour tour, most of the guests were extremely disappointed, feeling they had been duped and expressing it in so many colorful four-letter words and wanting their money back.

"This was a lot of bullshit!" exclaimed the young man to the group, "I don't believe in ghosts!"

"My apologies!" said the tour guide, laughing hysterically as he faded before their eyes.

His father wanted to know why his son didn't want to be the engineer he had wanted him to be. Was there something wrong with living a life well respected by society? The father set-up connections to architectural firms upon his son's graduation.

"I didn't work hard all my life for nothing. I struggled to make sure he wouldn't have to, that there'd be a safety net for him, for all my children," he told himself.

Still, his son put his engineering career aside for painting, a prerequisite course he took and fell in love with art. His father refused to accept art as a convenient means of making a living. He considered it a momentary, fleeting diversion that would pass with time or should it stay, become relegated to a hobby.

He went to his son's studio and found him working on a canvas, "So this is how you intend to make a living for the rest of your life?"

His son put down the canvas, poured his father and himself a cup of coffee, sat down on his stool, "Dad, I have no intention of making a living, I'm making a life!"

His father put the coffee down, "What?"

"Dad, when I was born, was there a memo or sticker attached to my ass telling you to work your butt off so that I wouldn't have to. Or did you just assume to plan my life without my input, without knowing the 'me' who was your son?

"Life's a struggle, and I'm not scared of it, Dad! You and Mom gave me enough to not be afraid of flying, of leaving the nest. You are your man; I am mine. I love you enough to love who I am."

His father realized the safety net was his son.

XLIX

The town's small population would gather in the morning to remember the life of the running back, James Huskus of Clairmont Community College, who died 35 years ago.

Little Timmy Henderson wanted to know why the memorial service?

"Strange tale," his father said, "James caught a one-handed catch that won the annual game giving Clairmont a state trophy. But he was seriously hurt, and for some damn reason, that play would be the only play he could ever remember and the only thing he ever talked about since his injury. We all loved him, but some days he could get on your last nerve, a nuisance, repeating that play a thousand times or more.

"Yeah, a real nuisance until the day they came."

"Who, Daddy, who came?"

"Four strangers from the sky. They corralled all of the town's people in the school's gymnasium, killing a few who didn't do as they demanded. They captured poor James as well. They apparently wanted something, but the rest of us were either too scared to speak or just didn't know, not James, though. He kept talking about how he ran his play, drawing them x's and o's. Telling them, he knew how to win and where to go and for them to follow him. I guess because he spoke up and didn't seem afraid of them, they followed him. They must have felt he knew what they wanted.

"Well, he led them to the old abandoned mine shaft outside of town, and once they were all deep inside, he smashed into a support pillar, causing a cave-in, killing all of them along with himself. It seems he knew enough after all."

After the memorial service, Timmy went up to read the headstone, "James Huskus, whose winning ways saved us all."

L

He stood before me, so tall I couldn't see his face, even though I was standing as well. His voice was surprisingly gentle for one so huge, and it seemed to cover the entire space around me.

"Why do you live with such limitations placed upon yourselves? You say your God is eternal, infinite, but you see yourselves as finite when you hold an aspect of God within you—Life! Life is an aspect of God, not of man; therefore, if God is eternal—life is eternal.

"You spend your lives placing boundaries, if not on yourselves, then on others. Do you not appreciate the gift you hold inside you? It is not a sin to be born, but rather a blessing to receive the gift from a source of love you could never truly understand.

"All is interconnected; your ego is a gift to make you 'feel' separated, not 'be' separated; otherwise, the Awe of Life and its interdependence would be too overwhelming. To know thyself is to be immersed where ego may not enter.

"You even limit God with a gender; we use OA, meaning the Eternal Mystery, the Undefinable.

"Most of you worship through a desire for reward (Heaven) or fear of punishment (Hell), not out of love. And were there no Heaven, would you still love God? Nothing is ever lost, break the vessel, and water is still water, and life is still life.

"You judge to find faults, not similarities. You grade to degrade each other. You waste the gift; you limit yourselves. You are more than what you believe yourselves to be; you are unlimited."

I awoke with tears in my eyes. I sat there; it was so real, if I were to remember anything from that dream, it would be "You are unlimited."

Story/Word Count
(For those of you interested in such things.)

Story	Word Count	Story	Word Count
I	115	XXVI	299
II	271	XXVII	272
III	294	XXVIII	256
IV	296	XXIX	299
V	298	XXX	299
VI	300	XXXI	300
VII	266	XXXII	277
VIII	274	XXXIII	256
IX	274	XXXIV	265
X	285	XXXV	297
XI	296	XXXVI	293
XII	297	XXXVII	299
XIII	299	XXXVIII	295
XIV	298	XXXIX	260
XV	294	XL	300
XVI	292	XLI	300
XVII	298	XLII	157
XVIII	296	XLIII	255
XIX	292	XLIV	298
XX	245	XLV	287
XXI	297	XLVI	294
XXII	300	XLVII	299
XXIII	198	XLVIII	300
XXIV	295	XLIX	297
XXV	288	L	300

About the Author

Amurá Oñaā came into this world pretty much like the rest of us. As for anything significant about him; well, that particular amuráti one day will be written.